# The Yoruba Story of Creation

# The Yoruba Story of Creation

## A Children's Story

Retold
By Ayodele Sasegbon

Published by
AMV Publishing Services
P.O. Box 661
Princeton, NJ 08542-0661
Tel: +1 609-627-9168; Fax: +1 609-716-7224
emails: publisher@amvpublishingservices.com &
customerservice@amvpublishingservices.com
worldwide web: www.amvpublishingservices.com

The Yoruba Story of Creation A Children's Story Retold

Copyright © 2023 Ayodele Sasegbon

All rights reserved. No part of this publication may be reproduced, stored in a retrieval system, or transmitted in any form or by any means, electronic, mechanical, photocopying, recording or otherwise without the written permission of the publisher.

Book & Cover Design: AMV Origination & Design Division
Illustrations and artworks by Rosalie Ann Modder

Library of Congress Control Number: 2023945057

ISBN: 978-0-9984796-5-1. (Paperback)
ISBN: 979-8-8689-3180-2. (e-Book)

*The Yoruba are a cosmopolitan people from West Africa. They have a rich history and culture expressed through songs, stories and poetry. These art forms are deeply embedded into their culture and they are one of the few people amongst whom poetry is passed down the generations in a hereditary fashion serving to chronicle each family's achievements, foibles and hopes for the future. When born, each child receives a set of genes and a poem (Oriki) from each parent. Some may say the Yoruba are a people made of words.*

*Within the bounds of Yoruba land in Southwest Nigeria, Benin and Togo, as well as in the diaspora, there exist as many versions of the creation story as there are gods (Orisa) that make up their traditional pantheon. As many as can be imagined plus, perhaps, one more. The version within these pages is but one of them.*

For Bami, long-awaited and much cherished

*The Orisa of the heavens and the waters*

Long ago before the world was made, there were the heavens above and the endless waters below.

The heavens were ruled by Olodumare, while the waters were ruled by Olokun.

In the heavens and waters also lived many lesser gods and goddesses, the Orisa.

At the centre of heaven grew a large baobab, its trunk as round as the sun which moved between its branches and as tight as a new drum. Its thin roots stretched between the heavens and the waters, knitting them together.

For the most part, the Orisa of heaven lived in the shadow of the great tree and were content.

One day, one of the Orisa, the most curious of them all, grew tired of the heavens, beautiful though they were, and desired a new adventure. His name was Obatala.

He approached Olodumare and asked for permission to create land, a new place to explore on the waters below.

Olodumare was intrigued by this bold suggestion and granted him permission.

*Obatala petitioning Olodumare*

*Obatala asking Orunmila for advice*

Obatala knew what he wanted to do but did not know quite how to go about doing it. For help, he approached Orunmila, the Orisa of knowledge, of wisdom and of prophecy.

Orunmila listened carefully to what Obatala had to say, before sitting and casting the sacred palm kernels, known as ikin. Focusing on the newly created patterns, he looked up and with steady fingers drew lines on the Ifa divination tray in front of him. He gathered and threw the ikin again and again. Marking the tray each time he did so. The tray was carved from the wood of the baobab and existed partly outside the flow of time.

When he was done, his eyes carefully considered the symbols he had made before he asked Obatala to gather five items: a white hen, a black cat, a snail shell filled with sand, a palm kernel and a gold chain.

Obatala gathered all the items but one. For the chain, he approached Ogun, the Orisa of metals and the making of things.

Ogun agreed to help but asked Obatala for gold from which to make the chain.

*Obatala speaking to Ogun*

*Obatala asking the Orisa to donate their gold*

Obatala approached the other Orisa and asked for their aid. One by one they gave him pieces from the gold jewellery they wore. Each piece of gold was spun from the light that surrounded and poured from them.

Obatala gave the gold to Ogun and for four times four days and for four times four nights he constructed a chain.

*Ogun constructing the divine chain*

*Obatala climbing down from heaven*

Obatala took all his items to Orunmila, who asked him to use the gold chain to descend from the heavens, after which he would give him further instructions.

Obatala hooked one end of the gold chain to a wrinkle in the sky and began to descend.

Down and down he climbed. Down and much further down.

Eventually, he was suspended above the dark waters, within which other Orisa lived.

Orunmila, speaking into Obatala's mind, asked him to pour sand from the snail shell into the waters.

Where the sand touched the waters, land sprang into being. Orunmila then told Obatala to place the hen onto the newly created land.

*Obatala pouring sand from the snail shell onto the waters*

*The hen scattering sand*

The hen, as all chickens do, began to peck and scratch, flinging sand as it did so hither and thither.

Where sand was scattered, new land came into being.

However, being a chicken, the hen did not scatter the sand evenly. In some places, it scratched deeply and these became valleys and the deep places in the world. In others, sand was piled high and these became hills and mountains.

Obatala was unsure of the new land and wanted to test its firmness. Not wanting to step on it himself, he asked Agemo, the chameleon and messenger of the gods for help.

Slowly, Agemo climbed down from heaven and with great care he began to walk on the new land, eyes moving in all directions looking for signs of sinking

*Agemo stepping cautiously onto the newly created land*

*Obatala planting the divine palm kernel*

Once Agemo declared that the land was firm, Obatala clambered off the chain and as advised by Orunmila, planted the palm kernel he carried.

A palm tree shot from the earth and as it grew it matured, producing all the seeds of the world below each of its two hundred and fifty-six fronds. On reaching its full height, it shed its seeds. This caused more trees to grow and shed seeds. Before long, a large forest had appeared.

At the end of the first day, Obatala and his companion the black cat, set off to explore the new world.

For eight months and eight months again, Obatala wandered contentedly before he became bored. The new world was empty and other than the soft rustling of leaves, silent.

One day, while sitting beside a stream, he caught sight of his reflection and pleased with his appearance, decided to make beings in his image.

He poured water from the stream onto the ground and mixed it to make clay. Pricking his right thumb with a thorn, he let a few drops of blood fall into the mixture.

He then began to sculpt.

*Obatala sitting on the banks of a stream gazing at his reflection*

*Obatala drinking palm wine under the blazing sun*

As he worked, he became thirsty and went to tap a nearby palm tree. He drank palm wine, becoming more and more tipsy as the day progressed.

When he was finished Obatala called up to Olodumare in heaven and asked that he breathe life into his figures, for although he could sculpt them, he did not possess the power to grant life.

Olodumare blew life and heat into the figures, baking them in the process. As this happened, Obatala, tired and unsteady, went to sleep.

When he awoke the next day, Obatala saw that unlike what he had planned, the people he had made were not all the same. Some were taller, some had more hair and so it went.

Obatala was ashamed of his behaviour and loss of control and with Olodumare as his witness, he vowed never to drink alcohol again.

Despite what had happened, Obatala loved the people he made and their many differences.

*The new people building homes and planting crops*

*The Orisa of heaven descending the divine chain*

The very first town was built on the site where Obatala first scattered the sand from his snail shell. It was and is called Ile Ife.

The Orisa who lived in heaven saw what Obatala had done and were pleased. They descended from heaven on the gold chain along with all the animals and lived amongst the people of the new world.

But...

Olokun the ruler of the waters and her Orisa were angry. They had not been consulted about the creation of land or the later creation of humans.

They raged and, in their anger, the waters rose, washing away large swathes of land.

*Olokun and other Orisa of the waters furious at the creation of land*

*The heavenly Orisa and new people petitioning
Olokun and the Orisa of the waters*

The people cried out to Olokun and the Orisa of the depths asking them to be merciful. Hearing their pleas, Olokun's anger cooled and the waters began to ebb.

When the waters subsided, the people rebuilt their homes and all that had been destroyed.

And from that day onwards, the Orisa of heaven and all people were more considerate of the Orisa of the waters, telling them of all plans that involved them and asking for advice.

www.ingramcontent.com/pod-product-compliance
Lightning Source LLC
LaVergne TN
LVRC091352060526
838200LV00035B/496

9 780998 479651